STRAWBERRY FIELDS

By Boo Ladred!

OH
THE SPATULA!

MY CAR HAS POP OUT LIGHTS!
HEY THIS IS MY CAR, SPOD! AS IN SPACE POD!

YOU KNOW
IT'S GREAT
ALL YOUR UPDATED
TECH N STUFF
BUT DO YOU GET PAID
ON A SATURDAY?

OH OF COURSE THAT'S NONE OF MY BUSINESS, BUT APPARENTLY MINE IS YOUR BUSINESS?!!
RUN!

DO YOU UNDERSTAND THE PROBLEM HERE? NO ONE GETS PAID ON A SATURDAY OK?
CANDY
CANE

THAT'S BESIDES THE POINT! HALF THE PRODUCTS DIDN'T SHOW UP!
BEEP
SHHHH

MY CAR IS ON
FIRE NOW,
DO YOUR PRODUCTS
EVEN WORK?

NO, I DIDN'T
USE THEM
CAUSE THEY DIDN'T
ALL SHOW UP
THUS THE REFUND!!!

ARE YOU ASKING ME IF MY CAR RUNS ON LOW VELOCITY
IT WAS BUILT IN THE MILLENIUM! YEH! I RECKON YOU'RE HIGH VELOCITY MATE!

WHO AS THAT?
I JUST GOT AXED FROM THE SPEAKER BOX AGAIN!
I DON'T SEEM TO GET ALONG TOO WELL
AND WE NEED A NEW BOMB.

NO!

AND THE GEAR STICK JUST CAME STRAIGHT OUT!
WHERE'S SPOD?

IF YOU CALL ME A MANGO I'M GONNA.....

OF COURSE
I EAT MANGOS!
YOU EAT BLODDY
MANGOS!!!
SO WHAT ARE YOU NOW?
A POTATO?

OH AND I S'POSE I'M A CARROT THEN?!
YOU'RE A PICKLE!

THIS IS BULLSHIT!!!
TAKE THAT HEAD BAND OFF!!
YOU'RE NOT A POTATO I'M NOT A PICKLE OR A CARROT!

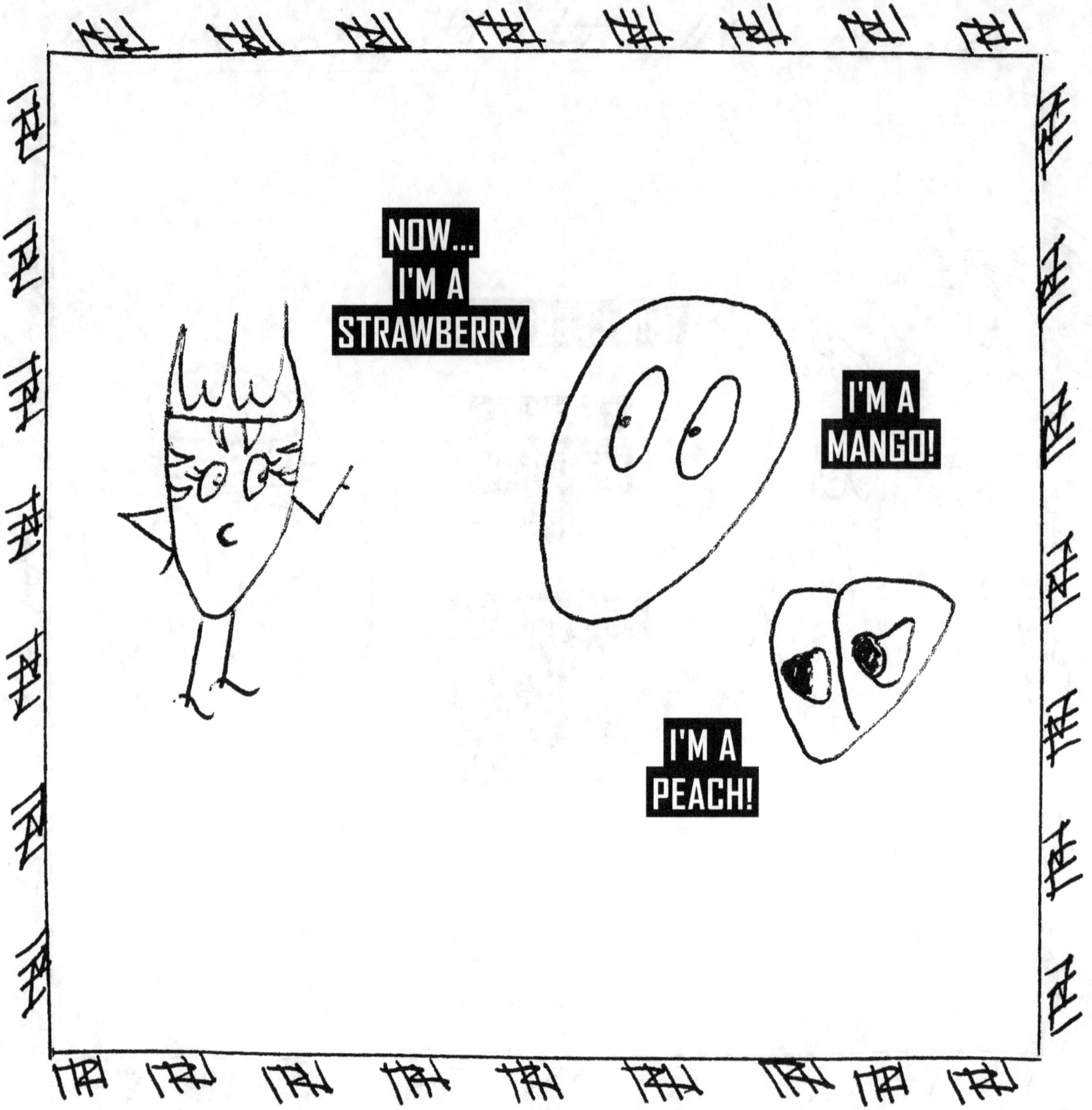

NOW...
I'M A
STRAWBERRY
I'M A
MANGO!
I'M A
PEACH!

SO HOW DO WE GET
A NEW CAR?

WE COULD
SELL SOME
PICKLES!

SO UR GONNA SELL ME FOR A CAR?
MOST GIANT PICKLE!
WE WILL SELL YOU IN A JAR!

WELL SELL THEM FOR $100 EACH
AND WE HAVE A BAG OF MANGOS AND A BAG OF PEACHES!
PEACHES
MANGO
34000
MOST GIANT PICKLE
DO YOU THINK THEY'LL EAT ME?

$34,000
MOST GIANT PICKLE
100
MANGOS
PEACH
AM I
A GIMMICK?
I'LL HAVE
A PEACH

WELL THANKS I'LL JUST BE OVER HERE
NOW WE CAN BUY A CAR
WE MADE $6000

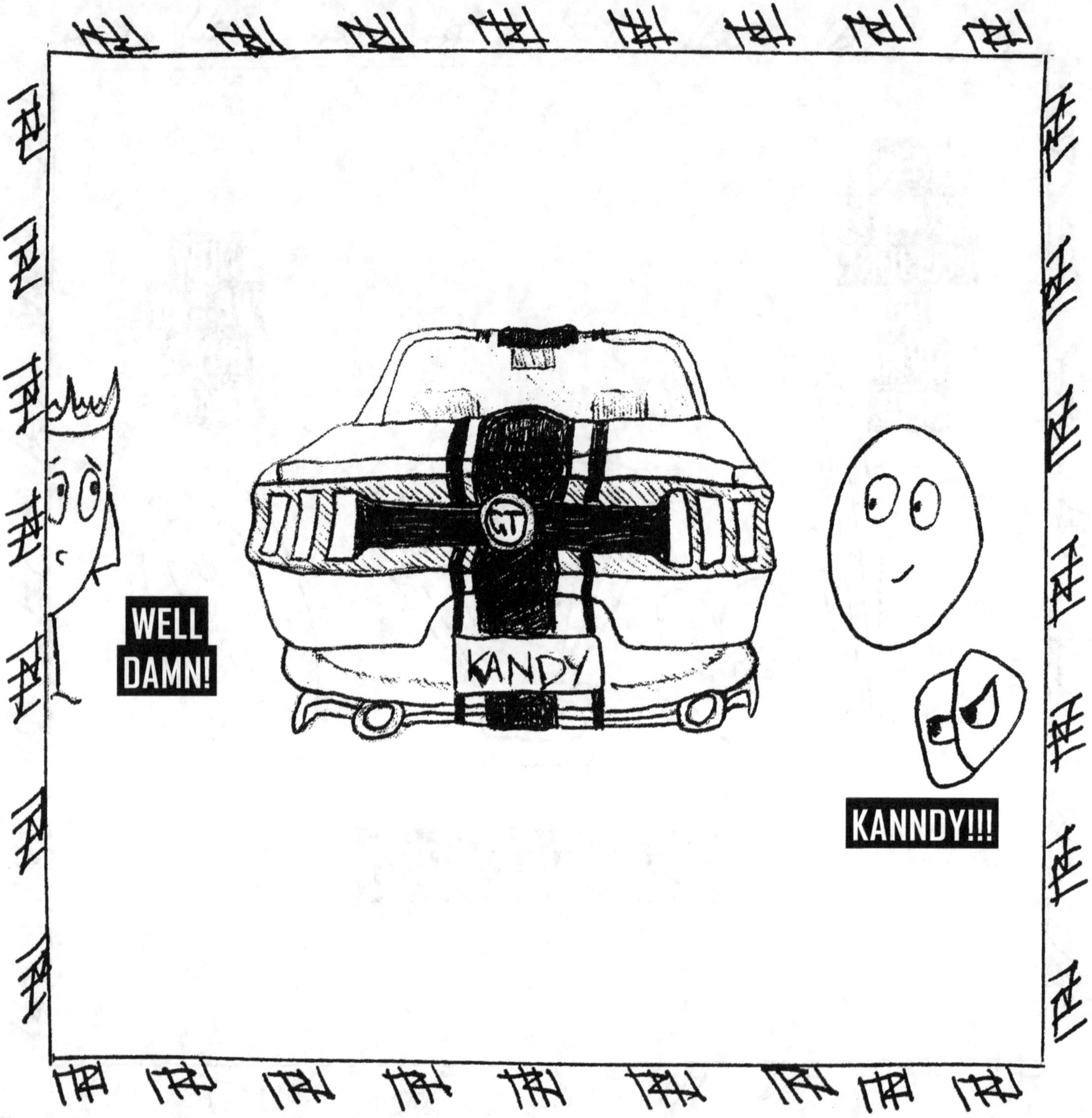

WELL DAMN!
KANDY
KANNDY!!!

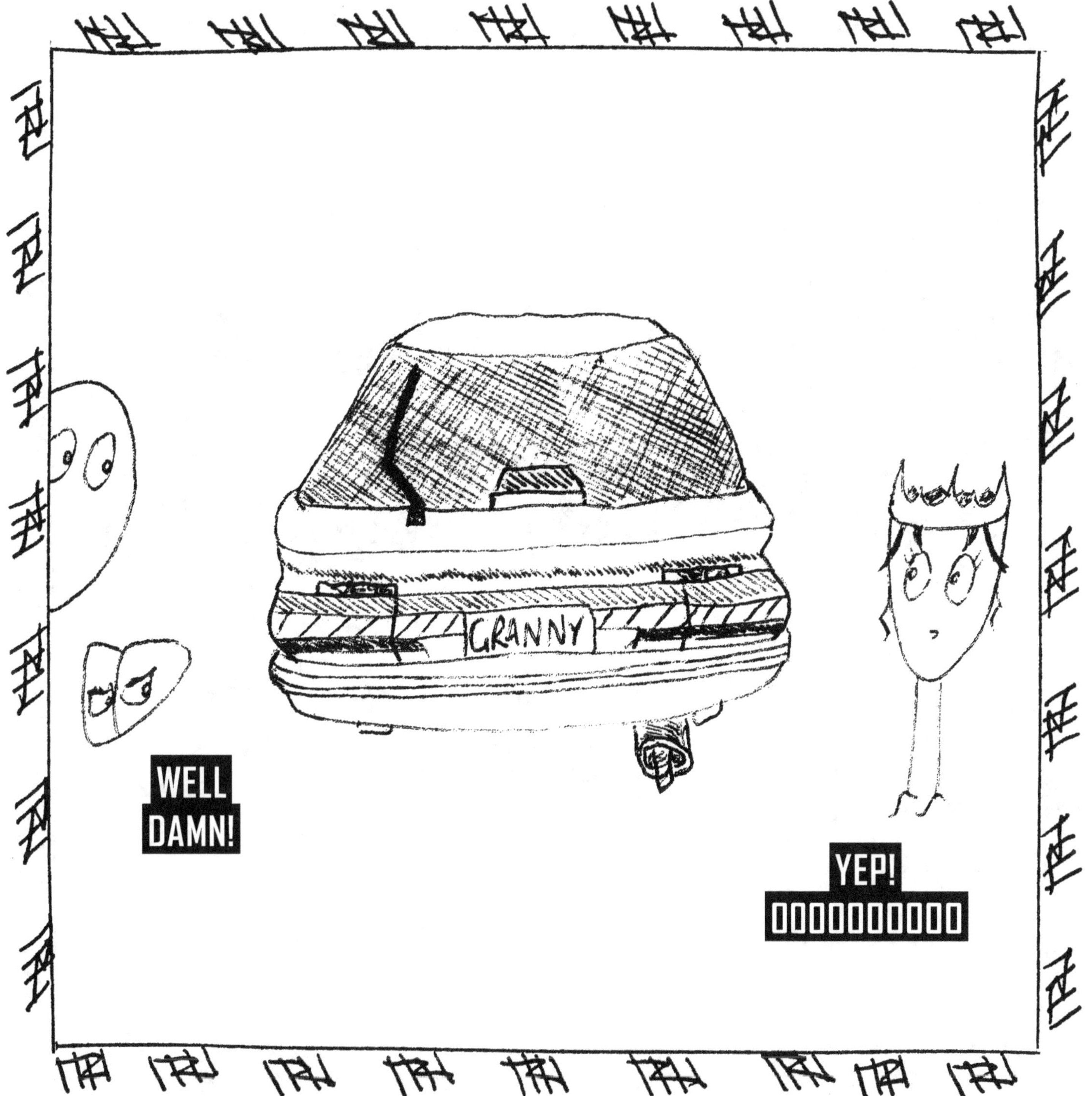
GRANNY
WELL DAMN!
YEP!
0000000000

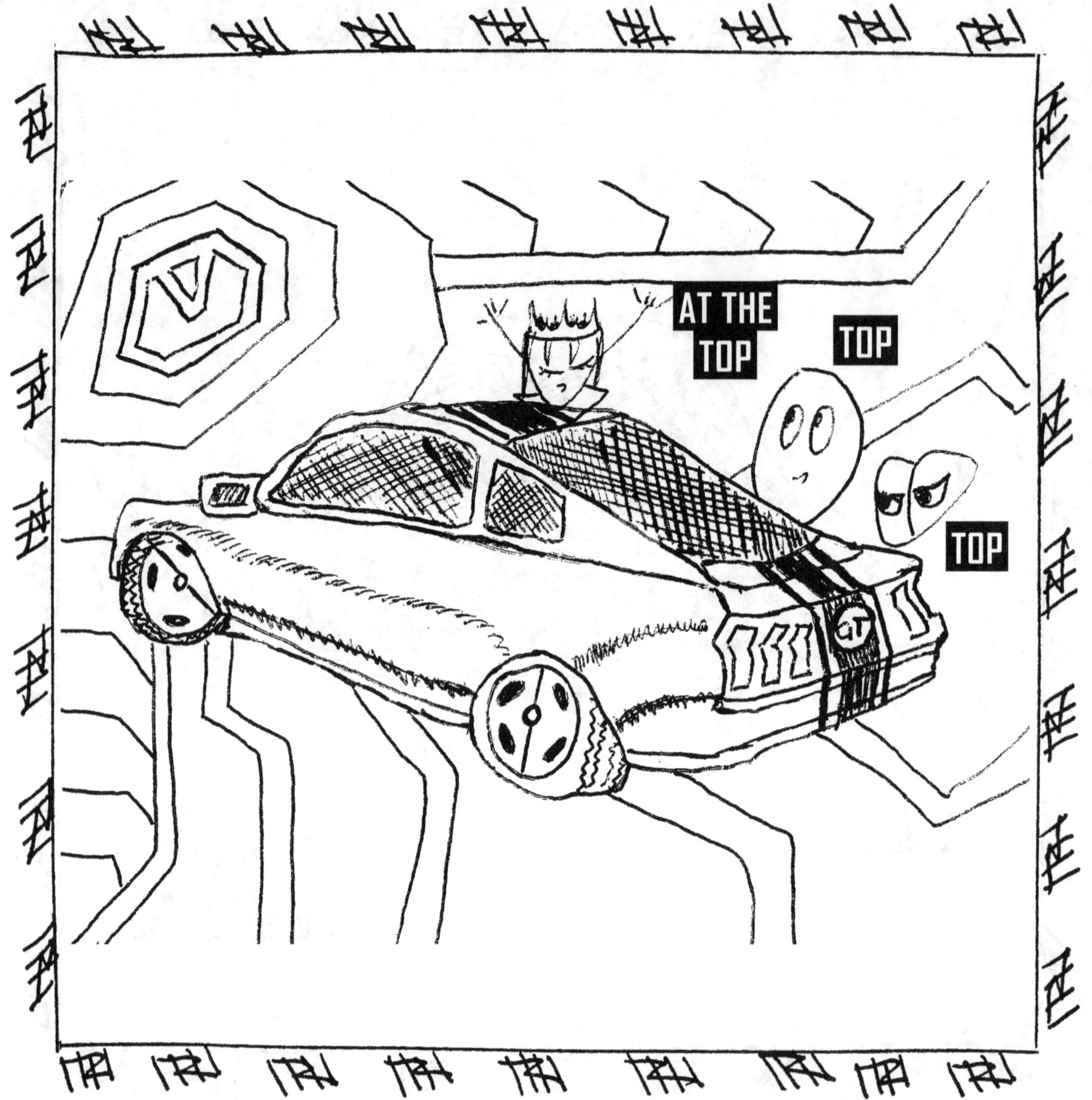
AT THE TOP
TOP
TOP

SUBS
AH YUM YUM YUM!
I THINK I SEEN THIS BEFORE!
YOU'RE A YO YO COOKIE!

SO YOU GUYS HAVE GOT SUBS AND I HAVE A COOKIE?
THIS BETTER BE A BLOODY GOOD COOKIE!

I SWEAR...
I'VE SEEN ONE OF THESE BEFORE!!!
ICE CREAM

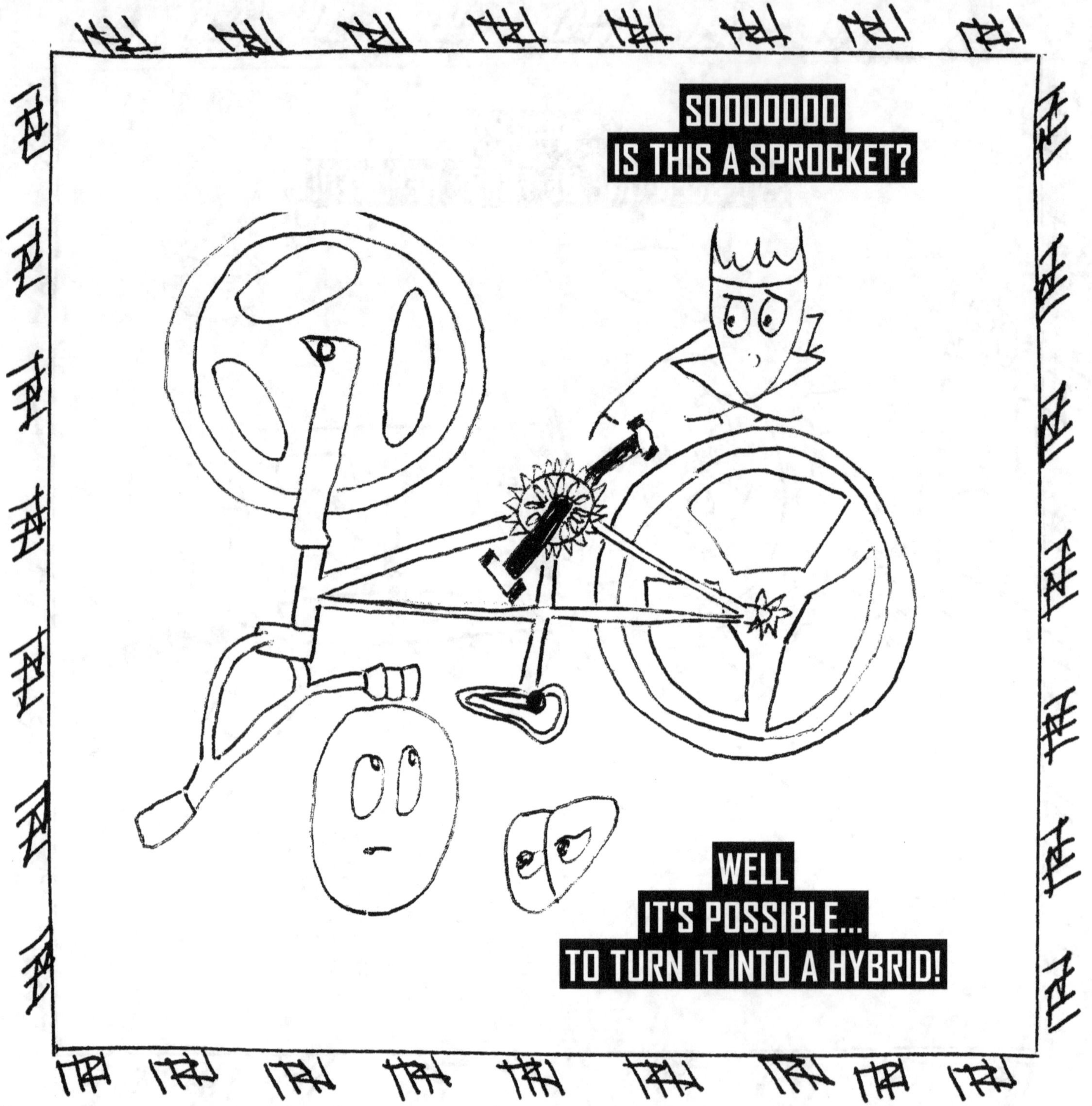

SOOOOOOO
IS THIS A SPROCKET?
WELL
IT'S POSSIBLE...
TO TURN IT INTO A HYBRID!

OK, I GET IT
BUT IT WOULD STILL LOOK COOL.
WHY DO THE CHAINS COME IN DIFFERENT
COLOURS ON SOME AND
NOT OTHERS?

SAY WE DID PUT A SPROCKET ON A COG?
OR SOMEONE DID...
THE DAMN PICKLE SQUAD WOULDN'T HAVE A BAR OF IT!

I HATE TALKING TO MYSELF!

WHO'S EVER HEARD OF A CLUTCH CABLE BREAKING?
AND I WAS DRIVING AND THE CLUTCH PEDAL JUST WENT STRAIGHT TO THE FLOOR!

STRAWBERRY FIELDS
WE ARE
NON-COSMIC

STRAWBERRY FIELDS
WE ARE
UNHUMAN...

STRAWBERRY FIELDS

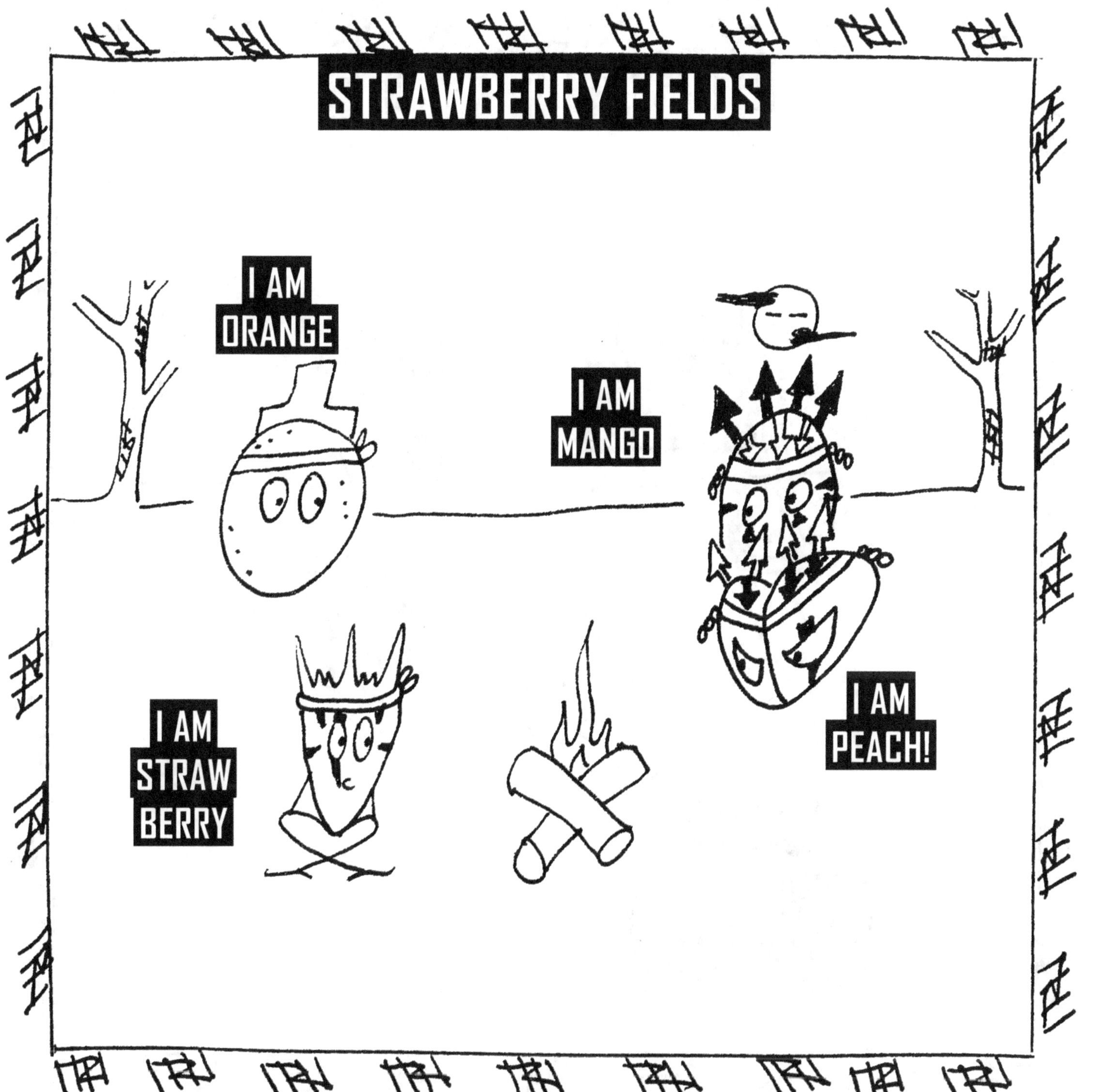

STRAWBERRY FIELDS
WITH THE ILLUMINATION OF THIS STICK
I INITIATE THE CONJURING OF THE SPIRITS OF STRAWBERRY FIELDS!

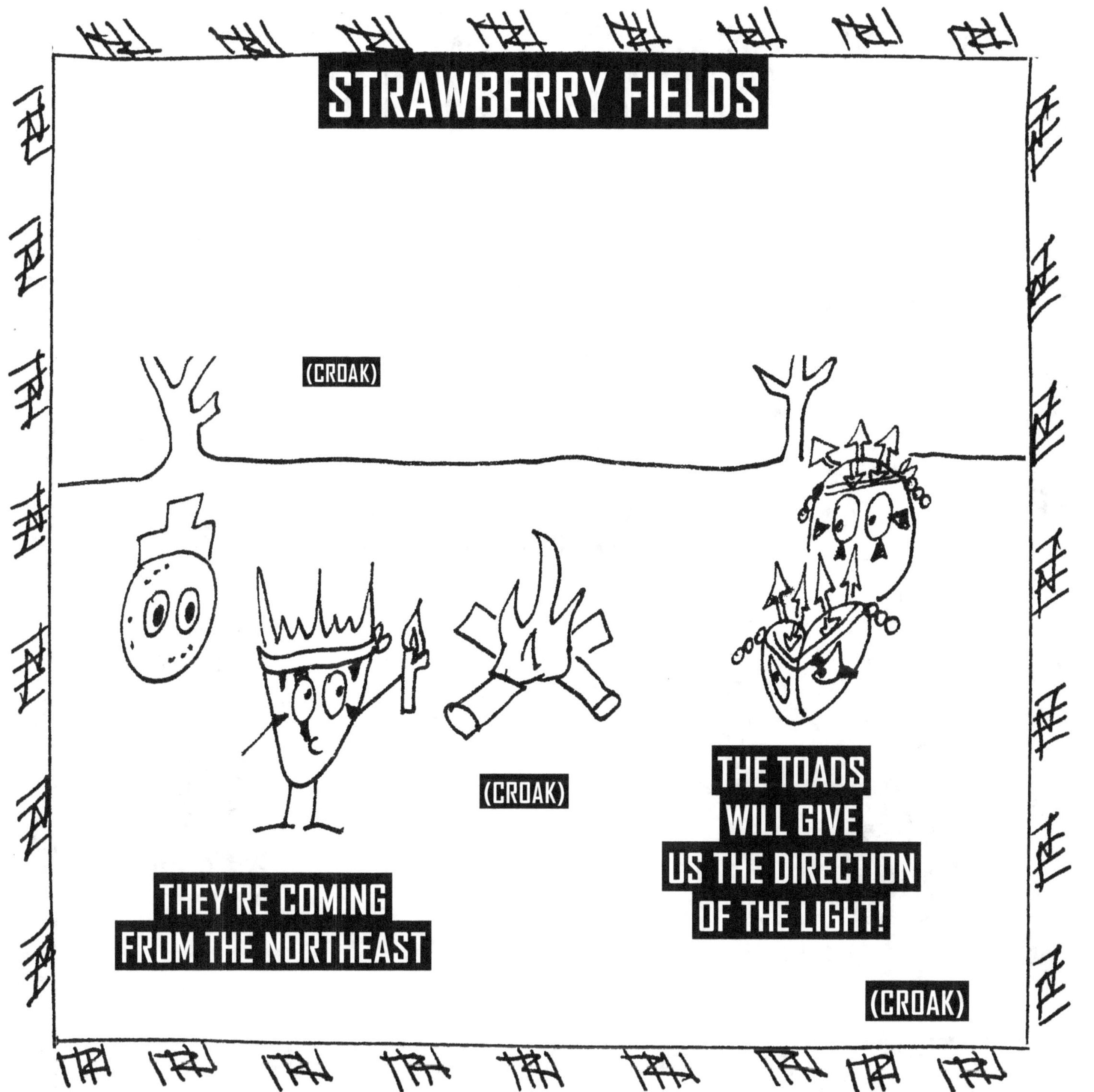
STRAWBERRY FIELDS
(CROAK)
(CROAK)
THE TOADS WILL GIVE US THE DIRECTION OF THE LIGHT!
THEY'RE COMING FROM THE NORTHEAST
(CROAK)

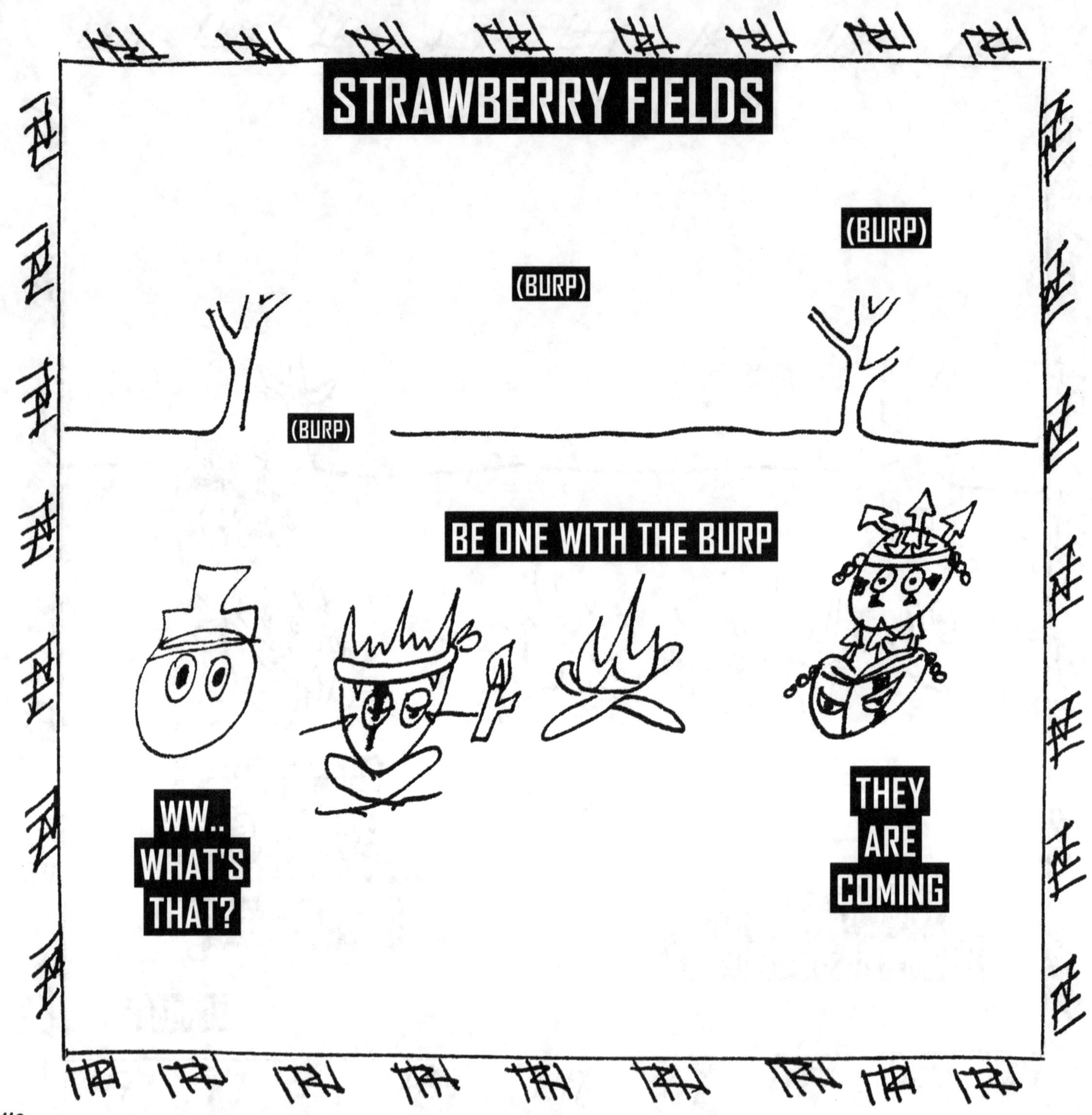
STRAWBERRY FIELDS
(BURP)
(BURP)
(BURP)
BE ONE WITH THE BURP
WW..
WHAT'S
THAT?
THEY
ARE
COMING

STRAWBERRY FIELDS

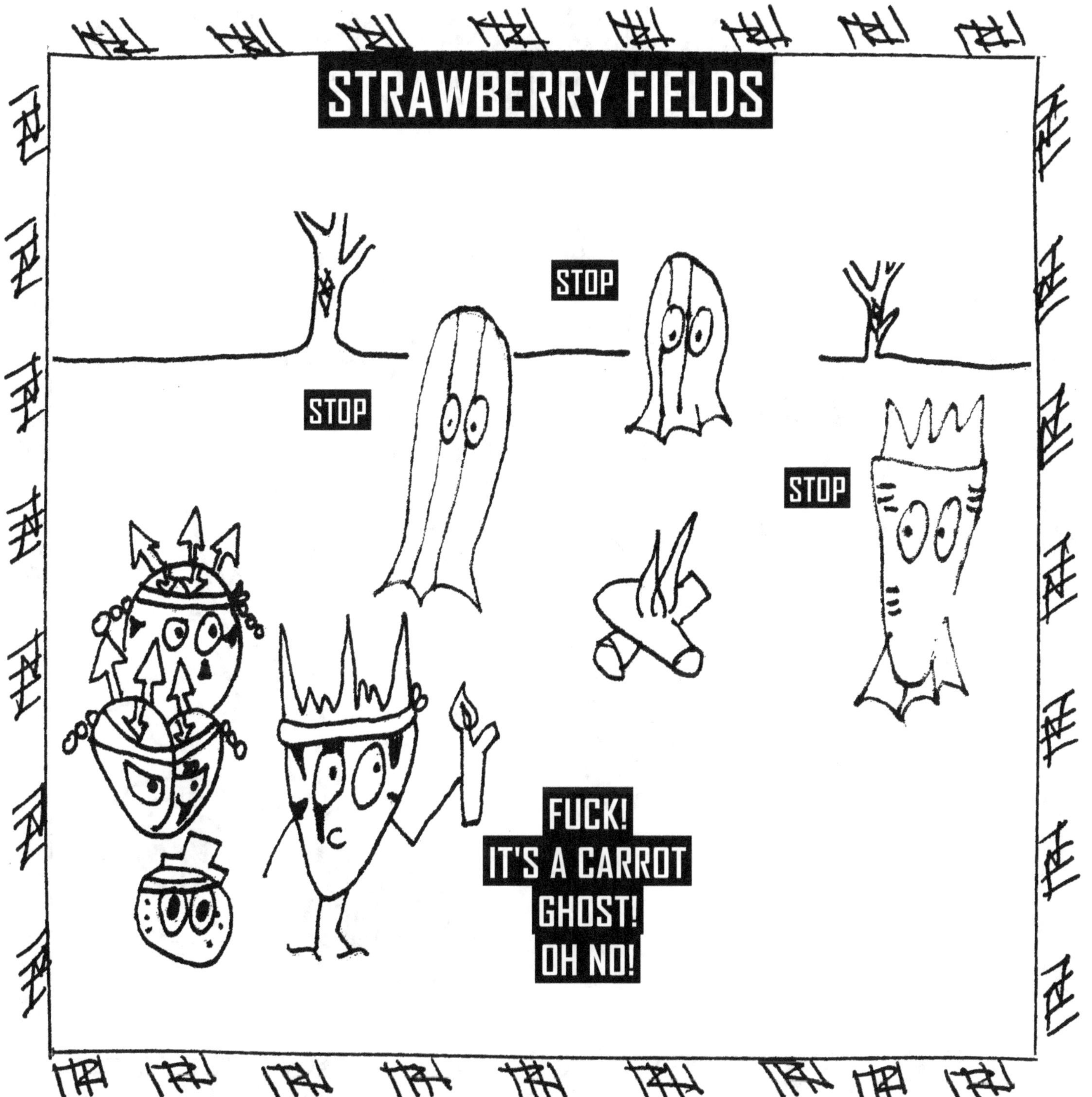

STRAWBERRY FIELDS

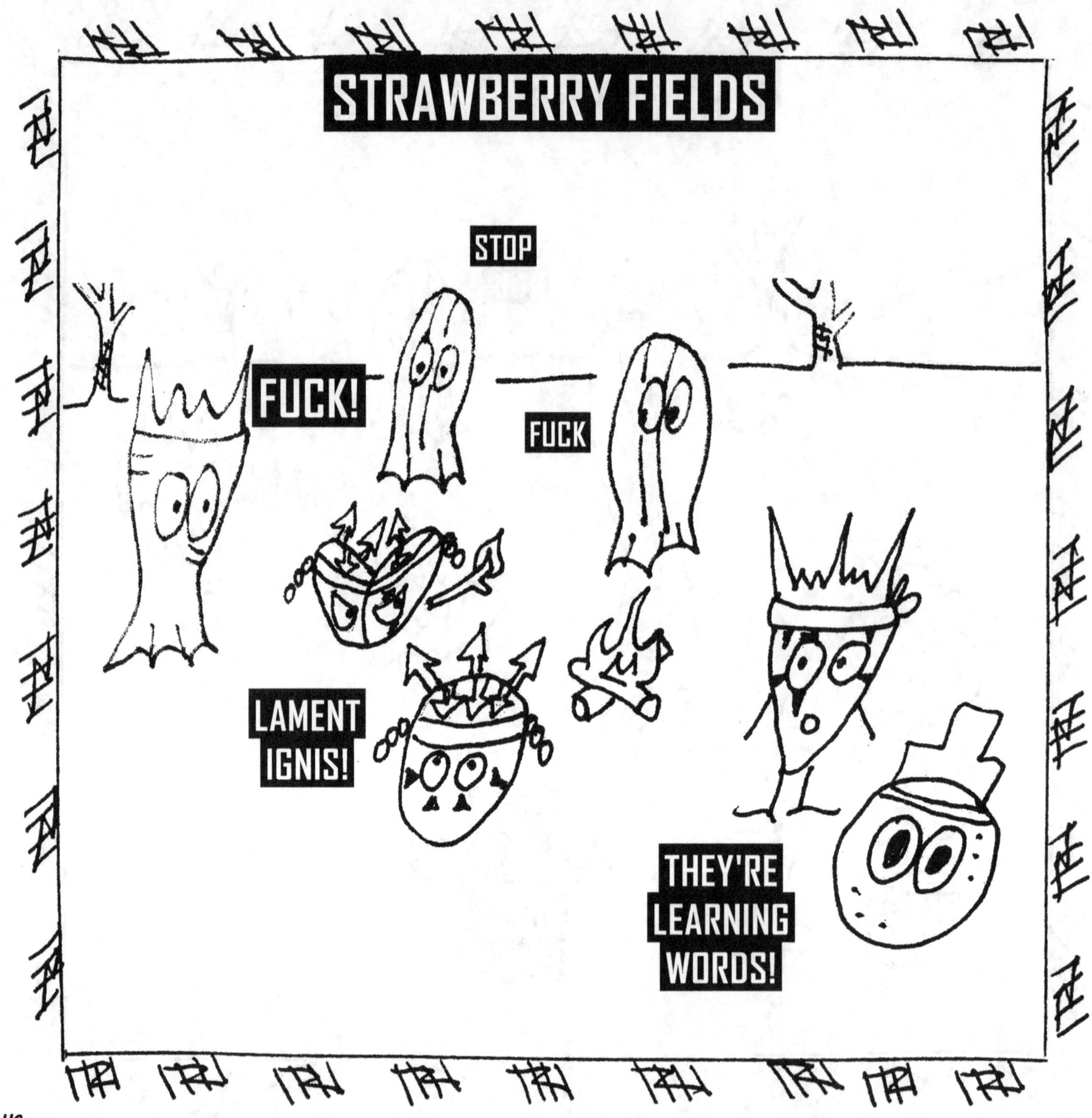

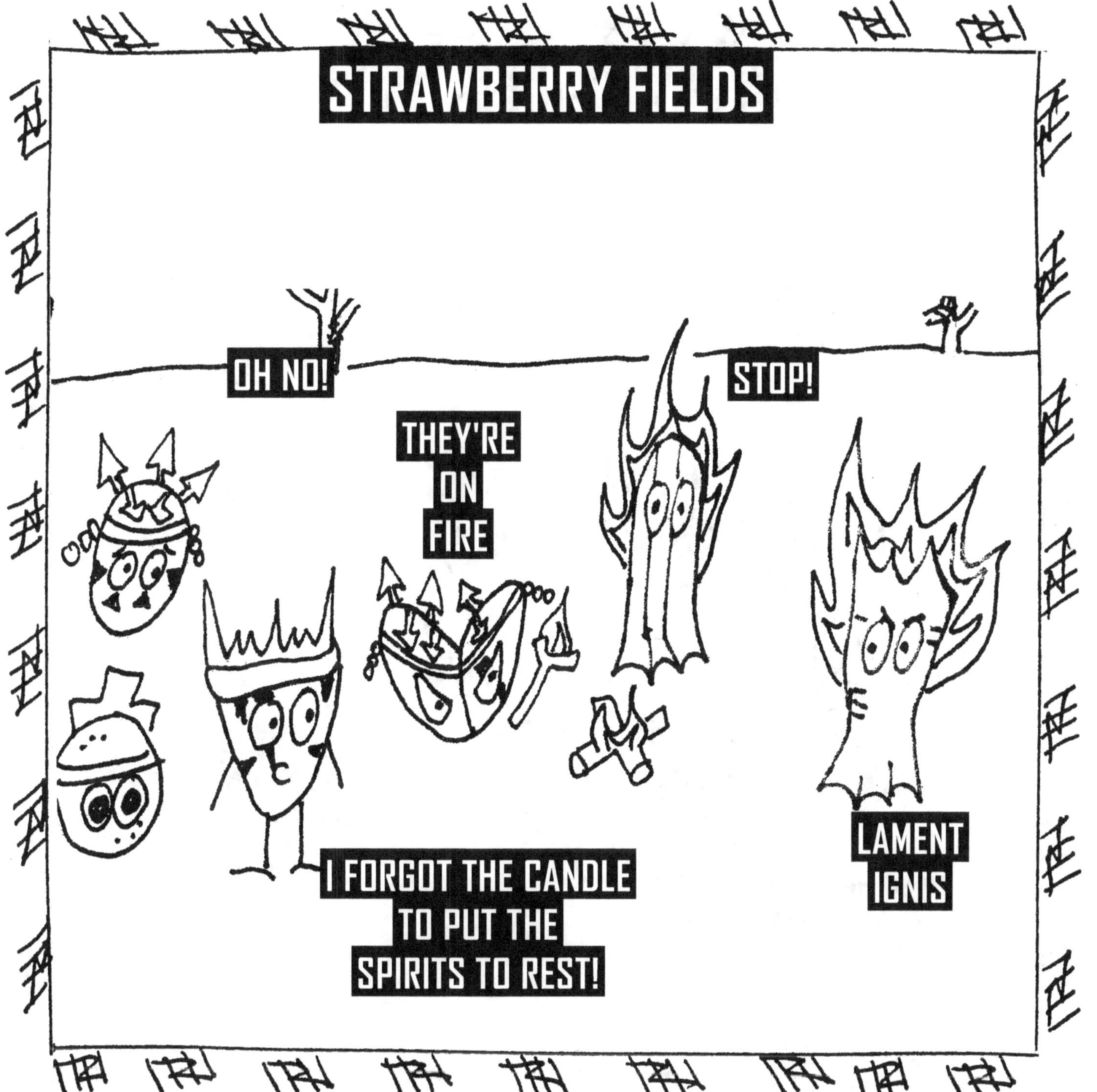

STRAWBERRY FIELDS
OH NO!
THEY'RE ON FIRE
STOP!
I FORGOT THE CANDLE TO PUT THE SPIRITS TO REST!
LAMENT IGNIS

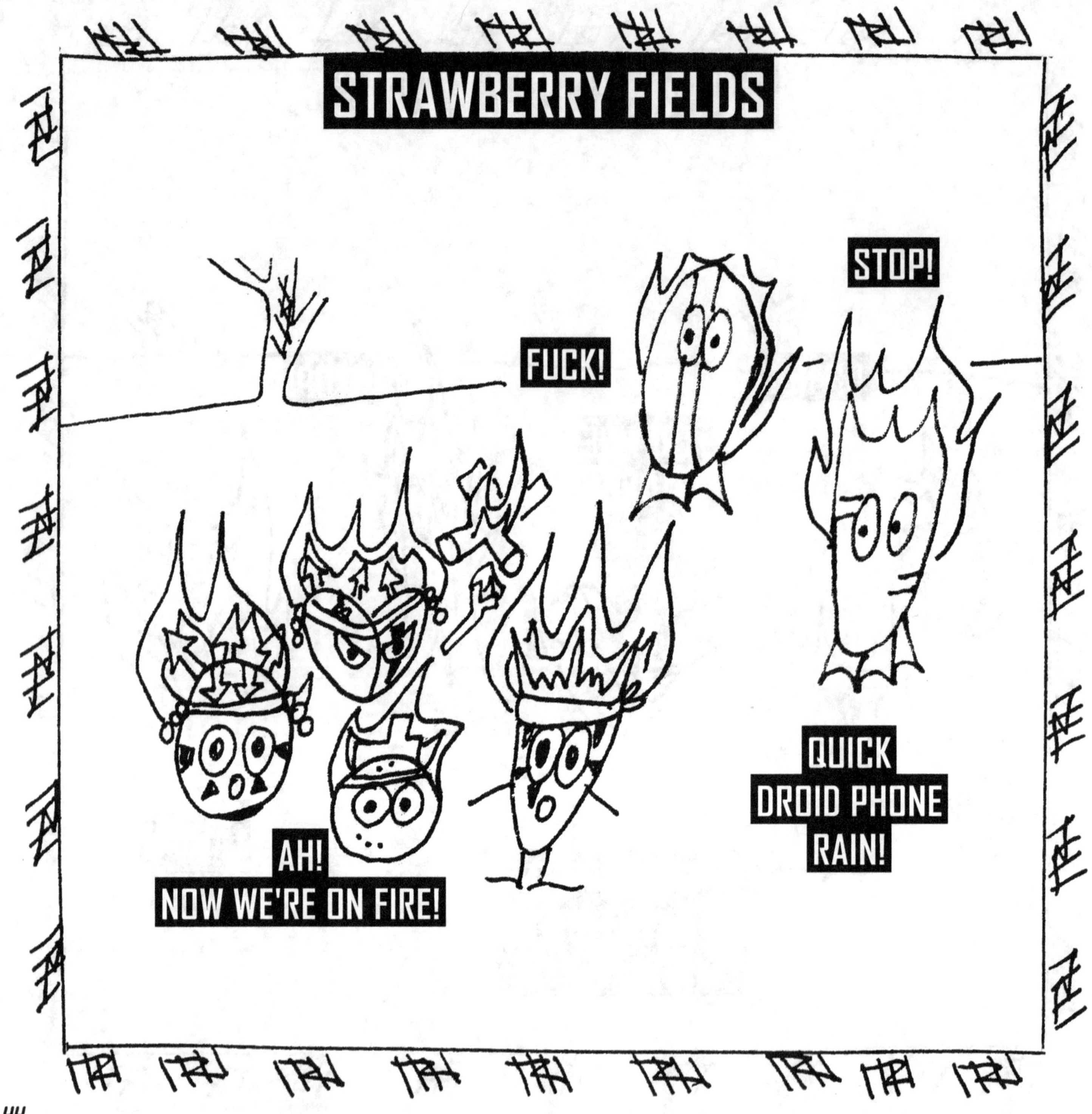

STRAWBERRY FIELDS
FUCK!
STOP!
QUICK DROID PHONE RAIN!
AH!
NOW WE'RE ON FIRE!

STRAWBERRY FIELDS
PHEW!

SEND THEM TO THE LIGHT
THEY WERE GETTING TOO CLOSE
WHY'D YOU SET THEM ON FIRE?

SACRAFICIAL!
I THINK WE MAY HAVE FRIGHTENED ORANGE!

ORANGE DIDN'T THINK THE PICKLE GHOSTS OF STRAWBERRY FIELDS THAT GOT SLAUGHTERED IN THE HAY FIELDS WERE REAL
HE PROBS WON'T BE BACK FOR THE NEXT ONE!

WE ARE S'POSED TO BE LETTING THEM PASS TO THE LIGHT SO WE CAN GROW HAY AGAIN
JUST WAIT TIL WE SHOW HIM ALL THE FERNS THAT GREW WHERE THE HAY FIELD WAS
LIGHT HAS TO PASS THROUGH WOOD FIRST

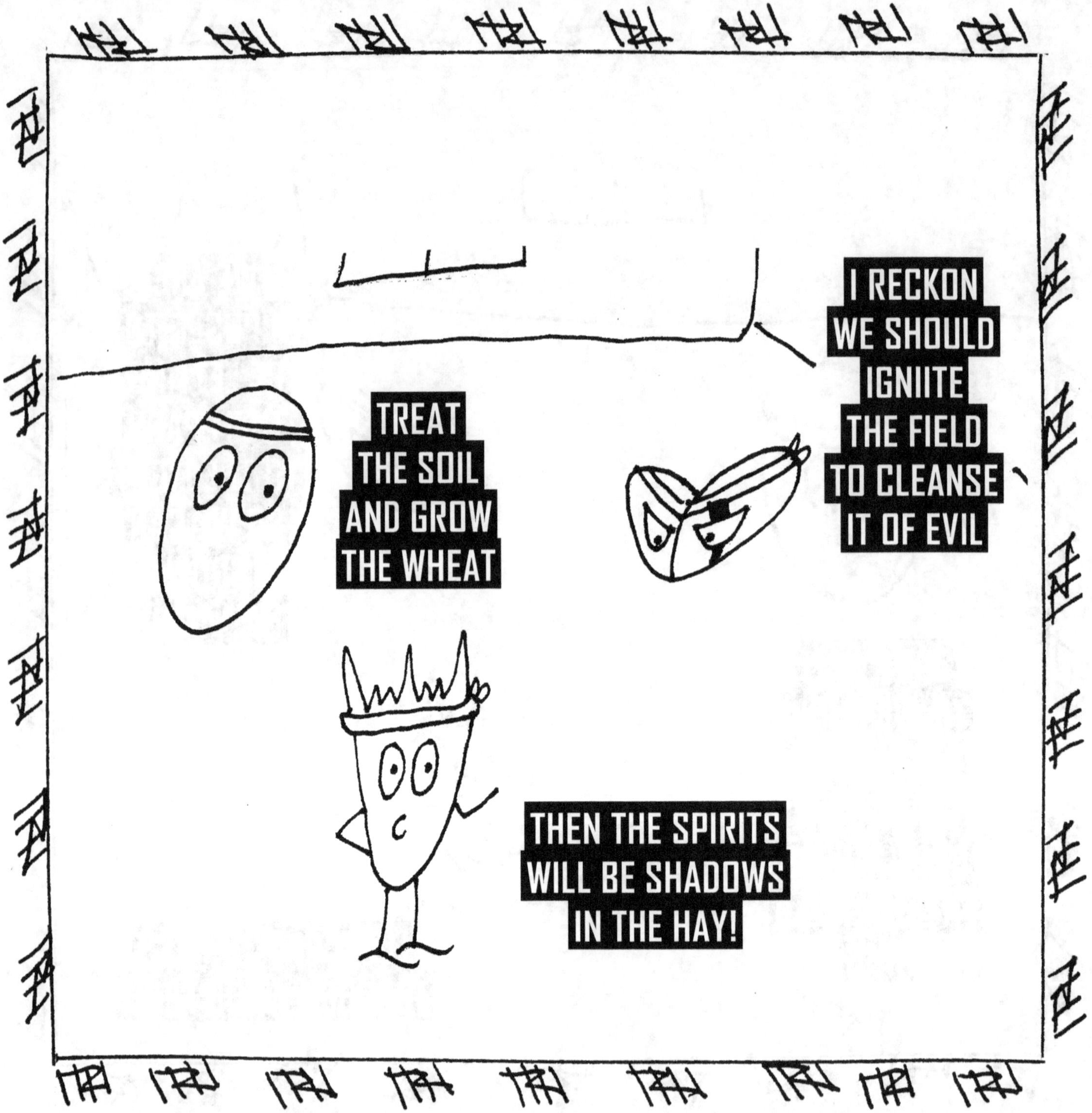

TREAT
THE SOIL
AND GROW
THE WHEAT

I RECKON
WE SHOULD
IGNIITE
THE FIELD
TO CLEANSE
IT OF EVIL

THEN THE SPIRITS
WILL BE SHADOWS
IN THE HAY!

NO!

SPOD
I PUT A BODY KIT ON SPOD AND GOT A BLUETOOTH WIFI WING ON THE BACK!
WE WERE BUYING A NEW CAR!!

BOO!
RIGHT! FALL OUT FELLA!
YEH! LOOK AT YOUR PANTS!
DO YOU HAVE ANY IDEA HOW STUPID YOU LOOK!!

SSSSS
ZZZZZZ
ZZZZZZ

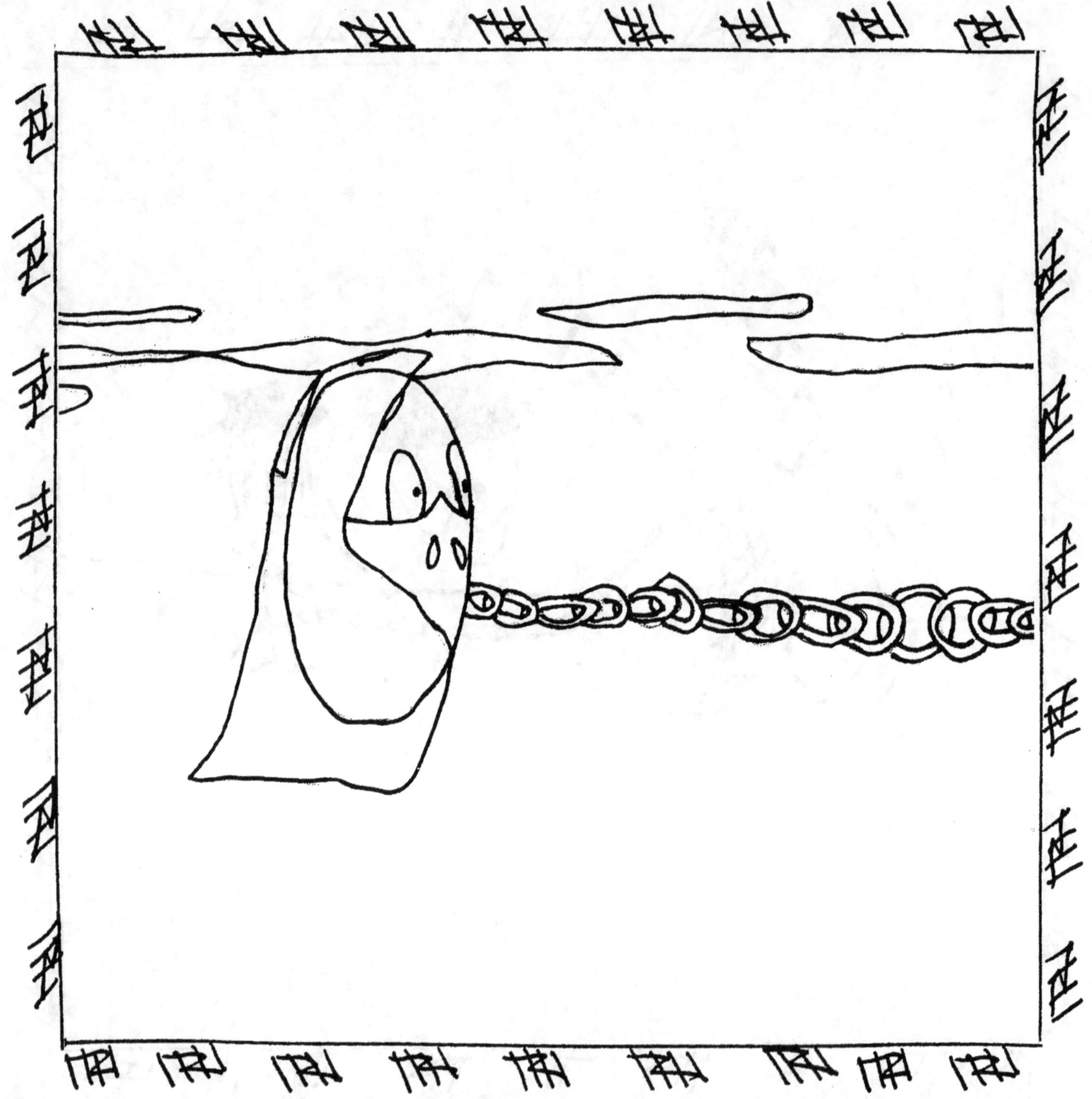

THE CHILDREN OF THE NIGHT AH HA HA HA
UH OH...
HOW?
1...

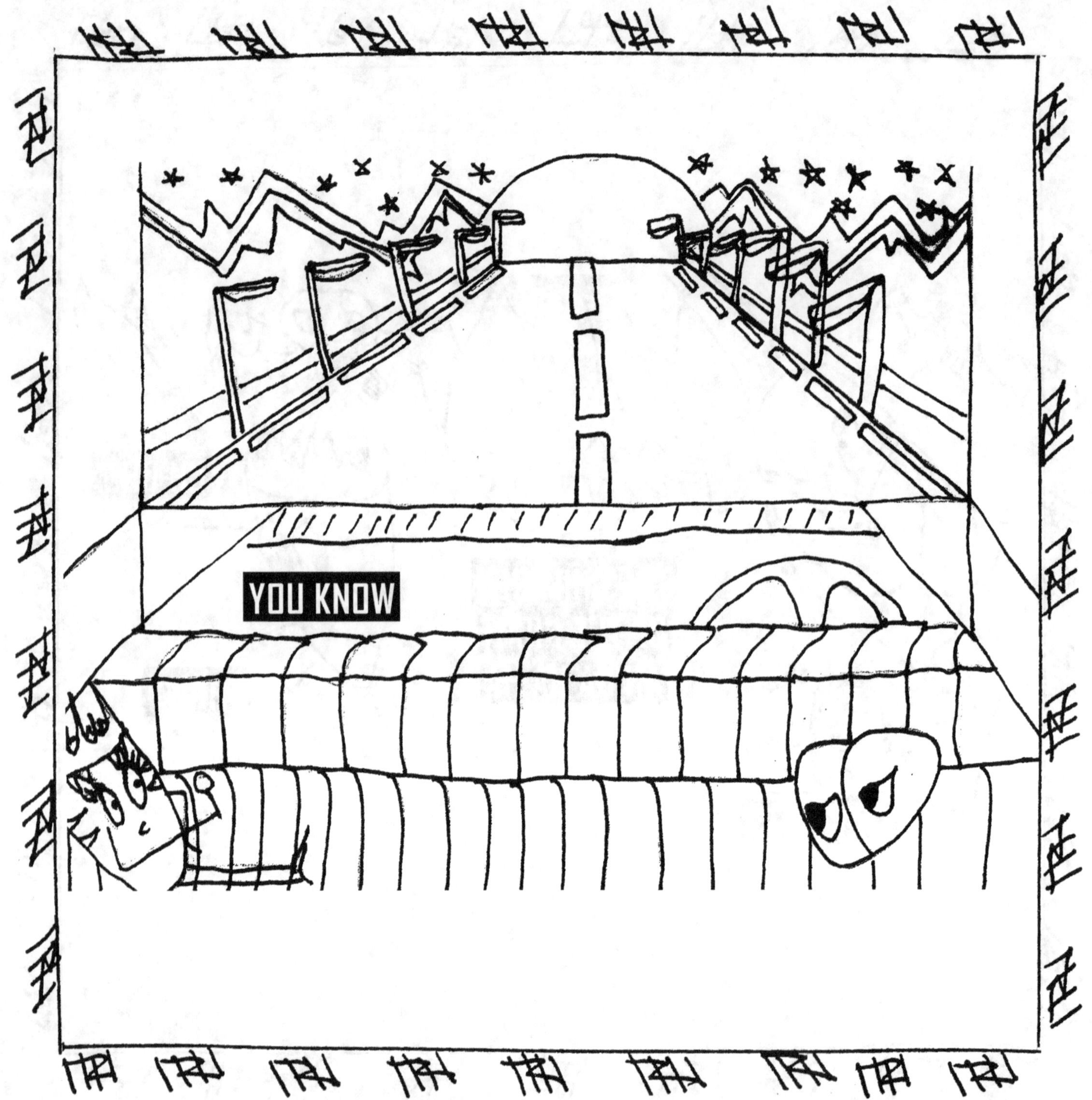

YOU KNOW

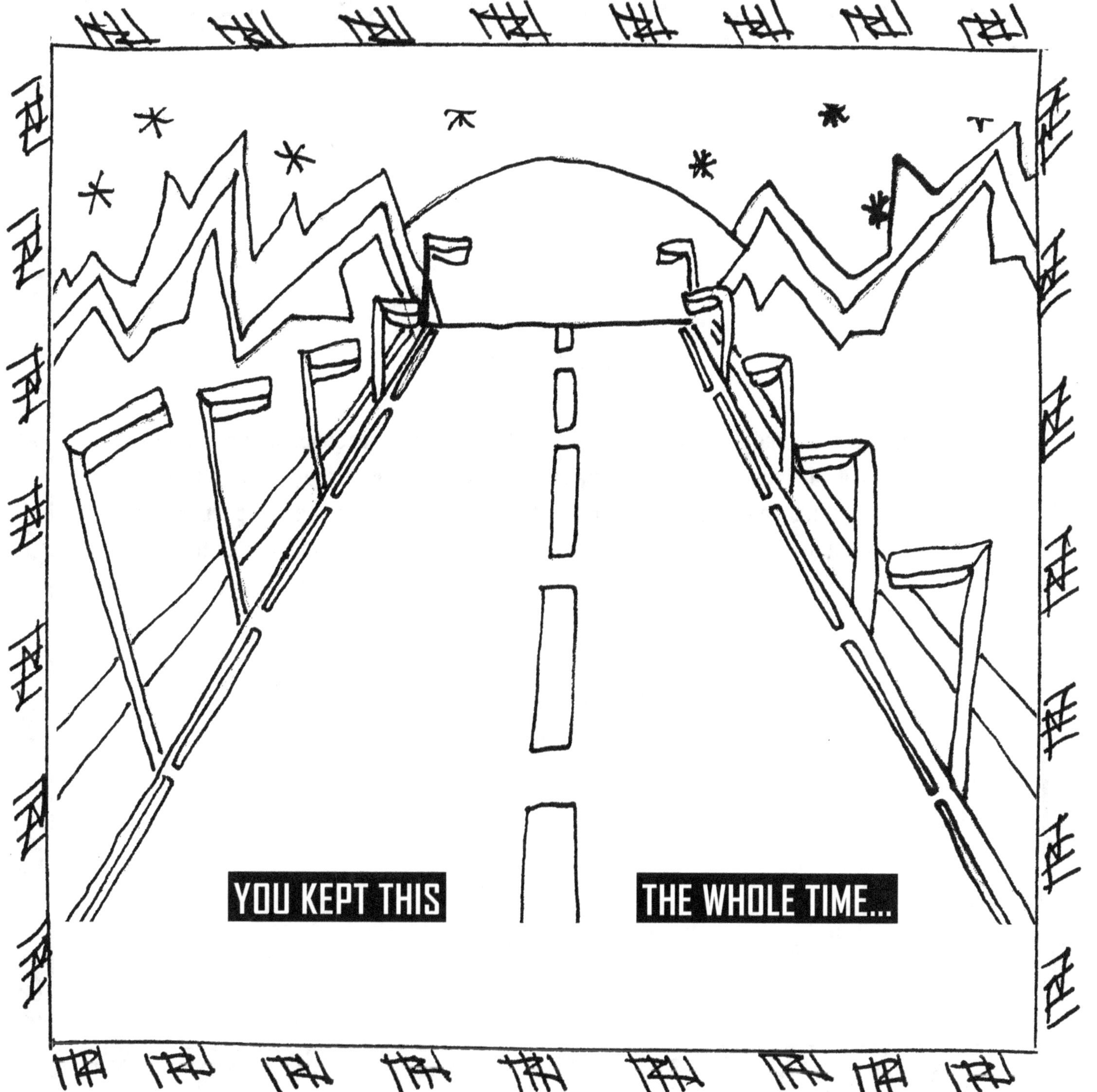

YOU KEPT THIS
THE WHOLE TIME...

Ladred, Boo (author)
STRAWBERRY FIELDS
ISBN 978-1-923214-23-1

www.ingramcontent.com/pod-product-compliance
Lightning Source LLC
Chambersburg PA
CBHW080352030726
47598CB00009B/2711